Foreword by Jane Gosney

Stella-Rose Benson is an artist working in Penzance. Her three cats are not only charming pets who inspire her stories but the models for her book illustrations. Her beautiful drawings of the Regency area of Chapel Street in the historic market town and the landscape of Newlyn form the backdrop of an enchanting story. The human characters have lives in the traditional local industries; the Jewellery Maker using Cornish metals and precious stones, Anthony a fisherman and Mr Side-Whiskers the specialist chocolatier. We are introduced to Sparkle Puss: a feline adventurer with magical powers. You must read on the find out how their daily lives are changed by the search for cacao...

©JGosney 2011

First edition Published 2011
by www.sparklepuss.co.uk

Text ©2011 Stella-Rose Benson
Illustrations ©Stella-Rose Benson 2011

The right of Stella-Rose Benson to be identified
as author & illustrator of this work has been asserted by her
in accordance with the Copyright, Designs Patents Act 1988

British Library Cataloguing in Publication Data:
A catalogue record for this book is available from the British Library

ISBN 978-0-9564402-04

ISBN 978-0-9564402-1-1 CD edition, non audio, 2011.

Acknowledgements and thanks to;

Thadius of 'Limited Fun'.
Mawgan at www.morewhitespace.co.uk.
My sister Liz - contributing editor.
Contributing editors; Jane Gosney, & Derek (from alongthewritelinesblogspot).
Bernard & Nancy - proof reading.
Digital Peninsula Network Penzance, where my drawings were scanned, and for the Adobe software course. Ben - Network Training Penzance.
Illustrations, digital artwork, and final editing by Stella-Rose Benson.
Bridgit Hollow Keen who made the original Chocolate House sign in Chapel Street.
My feline muses Insie, Mirabel & Palmiro – Insie was my inspiration for Sparkle Puss, and Mirabel intitially was for Myrrh before Palmiro was born. During the making of this book Mirabel produced two litters, Palmiro is one of her kittens.
Iian Scott - The enterpriseisland Challenge.
Thanks to my friends & family who follow my projects with interest & support, including Barbara & David at Books Plus Penzance. Thanks to the places & people who inspired this story, including; Salvador Dali.

Sponsorship – Thank you to;
Brigid, Liz & Charlie.
& Mike at the Penzance Station Café, 'Steamers',
(the purchase of 'The Life of Bryan', in Penzance Station cafe).

Written & illustrated by
Stella-Rose Benson

Sparkle Puss

The Cornish Chocolate Apothecary

Stella-Rose Benson

Sparkle Puss lives in the charming, Cornish town of Penzance, beside the changing and beautiful sea. Her first memory is of gazing up at the constellations as a kitten, and an entrancing full moon shining above the ancient abbey on St Michael's Mount. That night a Jewellery Maker found her on a silvery moon path and took her home - she knew she had found no ordinary cat and adorned her with a gemstone collar to celebrate her magical gifts and to keep her safe.

The back of their house looks onto some narrow lanes which during the summer months are overhung with prickly brambles and sweet scented butterfly bushes. A wall that runs beside the lanes is overgrown with ivy and grasses. A big tail-less cat, Manximillion, has managed to fashion these plants into a cosy bed for himself. He sleeps sneakily on top of the wall in the peaceful knowledge that nothing can disturb him there. Sparkle Puss has a little bed of her own with 'Cornish Treasure' sequinned across the top but nearly always prefers to curl up beside the Jewellery Maker instead.

Sparkle Puss likes to follow the Jewellery Maker everywhere and is often very playful and quite frankly also a bit of a nuisance when the Jewellery Maker is at her workbench. This morning she continues with a necklace she's making for St Valentine's Day and wonders who it'll be that will wear it? Just as she's about to sprinkle glitter on to a very delicate area of paintwork, the lively cat appears from nowhere and pounces, causing the Jewellery maker to shout.

"Right, that's it! Out you go for the day now!"

On this particular day for Sparkle Puss, being put outdoors seems to take on a sense of purpose. Her field of exploration has by now included wandering in and out of the local shops where she has become quite familiar with the townsfolk. She also has befriended a fisherman called Anthony in the near by village of Newlyn.

S parkle Puss
lives in
the
charming,
Cornish town of
Penzance, beside
the
changing and
beautiful
sea

and
quite frankly
also a bit
of a nuisance
when the
Jewellery Maker
is at her
workbench

On this particular day
her being put outdoors
seems
to
take on
a sense
of
purpose

It is a fine day and the twinkling sea beckons

*T*oday is a fine day and she fills her lungs with the fresh salty air.

"Hmmm wonderful!" exclaims Sparkle Puss.

At the end of the road she sees the sea twinkling on the horizon. It looks calm, just how she likes it and runs off towards to the sea front. Her journey takes her up Bread Street, briefly onto bustling Causeway Head and over onto Chapel Street, a road that will take her all the way down to the sea. The Jewellery Maker likes to think of Chapel Street as 'the Bond St. of Penzance.' It is lined with elegant shops and characterful Georgian buildings that are grand with pillared doorways or quaint and curiously small. Further on down the street is The Egyptian House with its quirky façade. Next door but one to that is a building with a plaque on the front explaining that it was the first Post Office in Penzance, before the first postage stamp. It now houses a different establishment altogether. A sign announcing 'The Chocolate Apothecary', hangs above the door. Here, organic chocolates are created by Mr Side-Whiskers. The right hand shop window is 'themed', with chocolate figures from Cornwall's Celtic and maritime past, and in the other are unique bite size delights in flavours such as 'Rhubarb & Succulent Rose', or 'Flosculi Sententiarum.'*

Inside, the shop's décor has been inspired by some Salvador Dali paintings including one called, 'Meditation Rose.'*

* See Index reference

On the counter, chocolate lobsters sit orange and winking while 'Mae West Lips' appear lustrous and drifting. Velvet seating offers an oasis of calm in which to sip hot, spiced or floral chocolate, topped with Cornish cream and a crunchy little meditation rose. Sparkle Puss often likes to nip in to the chocolate shop for a little treat and today is no exception. The door is slightly ajar, allowing her to ease her paw inside and push the door open. A gold bell dangling above the door announces her entrance into the chocolate haven bringing Mr Side-Whiskers out from the back of the shop. On seeing who his little visitor is, Mr Side-Whiskers momentarily disappears, and returns offering her a finger-tip of thick Cornish cream. Her pink tongue licks the finger-tip clean and she patiently allows him a stroke of her fur. After a few more pats on the head, a tickle under the chin and around the ears, she flicks up her tail with a pertinent satisfied curl and exits the shop.

Sparkle Puss has heard that the Chocolate Apothecary may soon be up for sale and the news has not been greeted well in the community. Mr Side-Whiskers does not own the shop and has been trying resolutely to find a way to buy it, but as yet has not unearthed an idea. She decides to return there later that evening, and realises she has been given a mission to save the chocolate shop - but how?

* See Index reference

*H*er
journey
takes
her along
Chapel Street
to
The
Chocolate
Apothecary

*T*o partake of
hot, spiced
or
floral
chocolate,
Cornish cream
and
a little
meditation
rose

Silk festival flags
made by
artists
edge
the
blue water
in ripples
of
colour

Continuing her journey along Chapel Street, Sparkle Puss reaches the Arts Club standing on the opposite side of the road. Here she climbs up the steps that lead past the church and through the yard filled with palm trees that swish their fronds and waft the sweet scent from their white flowers into the summer air. Standing still at the top, she takes in the panorama of the blue bay. The Coastguard ship is anchored a mile or so offshore, keeping an eye out for smugglers. After taking in the view for a while, she descends the steps on the other side of the church-yard and arrives onto the promenade. Silk flags edge the blue water in ripples of colour, made by artists for an imminent Cornish festival. Continuing along the promenade will take her all the way to Newlyn. Along the promenade seagulls are soaring and sweeping low, ready for a cunning swipe at a pasty from over the shoulders of unsuspecting tourists, sitting contented with their eye on the sea.

Half way to Newlyn, she pauses at the bowling green. Today the immaculate lawn is sprinkled with team members of the Women's Bowling Club. They are eyeing up the little ball at the far end of the green, eager to place their winning shot with their ebony balls.

On reaching the port of Newlyn, Sparkle Puss bounces onto the pier. A friendly bearded man is mending his nets with a rack of mackerel sizzling beside him. Reaching the end of the pier she notices a good deal of commotion where cameras are frantically snapping – three dolphins are playing in the harbour water, rising up on their tails and performing a number of acts for the appreciative audience. As her furry tummy is rumbling she decides to investigate the intoxicating smokey fish with the bearded man. To her delight he offers her some smoking morsels. Full and happy, she decides to tell the man about the chocolate shop and ask him if he has any suggestions as to what to do?...

        "My suggestion", he says, with a twinkle in his eye, "is that you look at the moon and the stars this evening".

    She gives some thought to this unexpected reply, and thanks him, but not before noticing a monastic robe hanging in the hut behind him.

    Before moving, on Sparkle Puss has a quick scan around for Anthony's boat, the Tiger Shark, but as she cannot see it she gathers he must still be out at sea fishing.

With its backdrop of ships and the sea
Sparkle Puss imagines Plymouth Hoe

He
offers her
some
smoking
morsels

She then turns up the narrow lane behind The Sea Cucumber Café. Half way up the lane she encounters Eulalia, the mermaid who lives on a wall. Her scaly and silvery green tail lies invitingly in the sun today.

Sparkle Puss gives her a friendly, "Miao", as she approaches and jumps up closely beside her.

The mermaid is a little apprehensive about the appeal her tail may have to a cat and tries to keep it very still and hopefully invisible! As the inquisitive cat passes along beside her she runs her nose along the lovely sparkly mermaid tail but she is not moved to bite! She understands, however strange it may be, that it belongs to a creature that presents herself as half human, half fish, and that she should leave her alone. Sparkle Puss decides to tell Eulalia about the chocolate shop and asks her if she has any ideas about how to save it? ...

"Look into the water my twinkly friend", she smiles.

Having finished her conversation with the mermaid, Sparkle Puss continues on her way. At the end of the town she hastens up the hill to view the harbour again in search of the Tiger Shark. At last she sees it moored on the quay-side.

The mermaid is a little apprehensive about the appeal her tail
may have to a cat...

After
a few
diversions

She
finds
the
Tiger Shark

Heading out into the open sea
with the
clear blue water
sparkling around them

When she arrives at Anthony's boat, all is quiet. She steps on to the gangplank peering down at the deep water below. The Tiger Shark bounces gently off the harbour walls with the aid of several pink and red buoys that dangle around the edge of his boat. A sudden swell in the water nearly causes her to lose her balance! A wobbly landing sees her off the dry side of the gangplank and on to the boat deck, where she cat-canters towards the cabins. Sparkle Puss sees Anthony through one of the portholes and taps the glass with her paw. Anthony turns to see a dark furry face with big amber green eyes looking down at him and climbs out on to the deck to greet her. Anthony has a Celtic tattoo encircled around one tanned muscular arm and is very handsome. His name is derived from the Latin word for 'Priceless'. And he is. However, his job is often a solitary one.

Anthony bends down to tickle her ears and offers to take her for a trip in his boat to catch her a fresh fish or three. Sparkle Puss purrs with a warm display of approval. Soon they are heading out into the open sea and cruising along with the clear blue water sparkling around them. After a while she tells Anthony about the chocolate shop and asks him for some suggestions as to what to do? He is just about to reply, when they notice a 'smack' of jellyfish surfacing near the boat and creating a formation.

"Aurelia aurita! – That's Moon Jellyfish, how strange to see them here", puzzles Anthony.

*A*s they both gaze quizzically into the water, they see that the Moon Jellyfish have swum in to a recognisable shape that appears to be of a large key to a grand door.

"This could be the answer to your question", continues Anthony cheerily.

"Your intuition has to be right, oh wondrous fisherman! I believe the key must belong to an eminent front door somewhere. A door that must lead to something very important," she happily concludes.

"Proper job!" chuckles Anthony, chuffed that he may have contributed to resolving her quest.

As the evening starts to draw in and the blue sky starts to turn a pinkish orange, they head back to the harbour. After her morning in Newlyn and the wonderful afternoon at sea, Sparkle Puss is ready to go home.

She passes the church in Penzance again, and viewing it from its elevated position on the hill she can see the warm glow of its coloured glass windows now lit from within. Rounding the bend of the road is The Pirate Ship anchored in the harbour printing T-shirts for tourists. Once into the town Sparkle Puss turns up through The Arcade. A street lamp at the top and at the bottom of the steps illuminates her way up past the dark shop fronts. She pauses at the fancy dress shop. Just near the top of the steps is "Ravens Textiles & Quilters", another curious shop that is stacked to the rafters with rolls of assorted fabric.

Through
The Arcade
a
street lamp
at the
bottom and at
the top
illuminates
her
way...

Stepping onto Bread Street she remembers the chocolate shop and hastily makes her way over there. Mr Side-Whiskers will still be in the shop making fresh chocolates for the next day.

Mr Side-Whiskers welcomes Sparkle Puss inside. Her acute detective nose immediately gets to work to help save the shop. She runs to the floor above to try and get a different perspective on things and settles by a window that looks onto Chapel Street. The Union Hotel stands opposite with its illuminated figure of Nelson shining in a dim porch. She then notices the moon is shining above the Abbey, which has to be a good omen, but what does it mean? She feels the moon is telling her to take action and remembers that a telescope stands at one of the attic windows. She races up there immediately and positions herself comfortably to gain a glimpse of the universe. She is rewarded with a spectacular view of the brilliant stars in the night sky. Suddenly a flying insect distracts her and she gives it a swipe – a cat can never resist such a provocative flying morsel, and in doing so, her paw knocks the telescope. It swivels away to the right and into the eastern universe. By chance or providence she now has an altogether different view when returning to star gaze. Sparkle Puss remembers the words of the bearded man earlier in the day and where he said to look this evening.

She now realises she's looking at something quite extraordinary – the telescope has positioned itself on the moon and the Jewelled Handle*. She can also see a cluster of stars called the 'Jewel Box'*. Her collar is sparkling and she understands the Jewellery Maker is guiding her to follow the signs in the sky. The moon is high above the town and leading a path to the town Abbey on the harbour. That is her clue as to where to go straight away!

She launches into a cat gallop on to Chapel Street where her speeding tracks are cruelly interrupted. The snarling voice of Manximillion, the tail-less cat, calls to her.

"And where might you be going, and in such a hurry my pretty twinkle puss?!"

A large weighty paw lands on her tail with ecstatic aplomb, and she turns her face to his.

"Ke tha gerras!"* She snaps.

Her swift and assertive response stirs the beast, enabling her cherished extremity to slip from under his paw. She seizes her moment to run. At the Admiral Benbow Inn she can see up on the roof top is the Benbow Musketeer – who for some 400 years has protected the town from pirates. He catches sight of and aims fire at the menacing Manx ... hearing a vanquished,

"Yelp!"

She believes it is safe to continue on her way to the Abbey.

*See index reference

Mr
Side-Whiskers
welcomes
Sparkle Puss
inside

The telescope
has
positioned
itself on
the moon
and
the
Jewelled
Handle

*A*rriving at the Abbey door Sparkle Puss notices a jewelled handle – shimmering like the moon.

"This has got to be the connection to the Chocolate Apothecary – what lies behind this door?" she wonders.

Purring loudly with anticipation she pulls the brass door-bell. Its chime rings out with a clear and joyful tone. The door is opened by the Abbot, who lowers his hood to greet her. She sees it is lined with a velvet rainbow, and she now recognises the bushy beard of the mackerel man in Newlyn! Soon after a handsome cat comes bounding up to join them. She deciphers some curly script around his beautiful furry neck as 'Myrrh'. The Abbot, on seeing that their little visitor is a cat, disappears back into the depths of the Abbey.

"I know who you are, and why you have come here," says Myrrh. "With gleaming fur like that you must be Sparkle Puss."

Myrrh invites her in to share his supper, and afterwards they curl up in the warmth of the Abbey.

The next day Myrrh asks her to follow him in to the Abbey garden where banana and lush plants surround a well kept lawn. A fish filled stream meanders through the borders. The fish look plump and happy, but she knows that just like the Newlyn mermaid they are special fishy creatures and are not for eating. After all, Myrrh would surely have made a meal of them himself by now!

"We've been waiting for you to come. Now what you need to do is tell us who it is you want us to help?"

Sparkle Puss realises she may have just taken the first step in helping to save the chocolate shop.

Myrrh continues, "Do you see it is a full moon? By making contact with us on such a day, you've enabled us at last to make use of the crop we've been keeping in store.   Further down the garden she can make out the tops of some glass hot houses.

"Come this way and see what the monks have been growing" beckons Myrrh.

A sign points to 'Theobroma Cacao – Luna Rainbowus, Organicus'*. As they enter one of the steamy hot houses, rows of plants with colourful pods appear amid the humid warmth.

*See index reference

This
has got to be
the
connection
to the
Chocolate
Apothecary
– what lies behind
this door?

With
gleaming fur
like that
you
must be
Sparkle Puss

Theobroma Cacao - Luna Rainbowus, Organicus

The monks
have
created
a special place
for these
precious
rainforest fruits,
here
on the
Holy
Headland

"The monks have created a special place for these precious rainforest fruits, here on the Holy Headland. By planting, growing and harvesting them according to the phases of the moon, they have produced plants with unique and delicious cocoa beans!".

Sparkle Puss now understands that these special beans could create the chocolate to help save Mr Side-Whiskers shop. She also knows that the Jewellery Maker will create some celestially inspired jewelled boxes in which to present it. Myrrh continues to explain to her that the monks grow their unusual crop in secret and that it must remain that way. Sparkle Puss is somewhat puzzled by this but Myrrh reassures her that gradually all would be revealed to her.

Over the next few days, Sparkle Puss, Myrrh and the monks work hard to produce the chocolate. Eventually like priceless bars of un-coined gold, they deliver them to Mr Side-Whiskers at his shop on Chapel Street.

At last the day arrives when the new, Moon chocolate can take pride of place in the shop window. Mr Side-Whiskers has arranged a party and Myrrh arrives with a gift from the Abbey monks – the jewelled handle.

Myrrh
arrives with
a gift
from the
Abbey monks
– the
jewelled handle

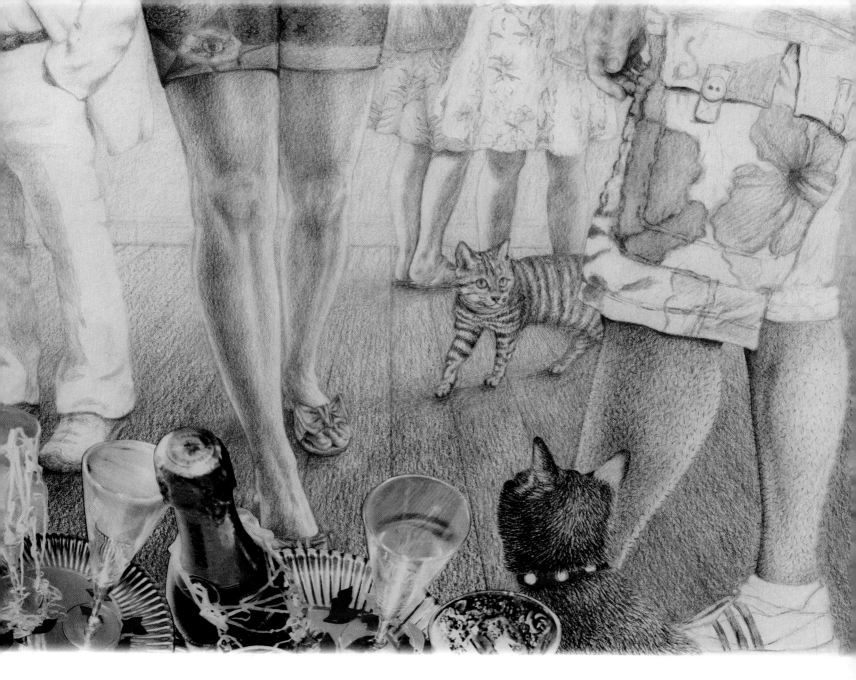

and nudges him in the direction of the Jewellery Maker

*I*t is not long before customers from far and wide start crowding in to the shop. The Jewellery Maker sinks into a velvet armchair to savour the new chocolate. As she does so, the chair wobbles about. She looks down at its feet in bewilderment and there she finds a glorious jewelled door handle fixed underneath.* By late afternoon the party is in full swing and Mr Side-Whiskers is thrilled. At last Sparkle Puss and Myrrh see Anthony amongst the crowd and nudge him in the direction of the Jewellery Maker.

"Second important mission accomplished!" She thinks, slinking off with tingling whiskers and a cunning grin...

For now, Sparkle Puss can return to gather glitter with the Jewellery Maker, make merry with Myrrh and find fish with the fisherman, knowing that their beloved chocolate shop is saved. The new, Moon chocolate is not only a joy to eat, but also with its brilliant remedies, has managed to inspire the disenchanted to live with more blissful beatitudes.

*See index reference

The new,
moon chcolate
is
a joy
to eat

Bleujennow
an lor

The CHOCOLATE APOTHECARY

Index Reference;

Bleujennow an lor - Moon flowers, (Cornish)
Flosculi Sententiarum - Flowers of fine thoughts (Latin).

Jewel Box – an open stellar cluster of stars in the Southern Cross or Crux, which is a cross-shaped constellation in the far Southern Hemisphere. The crux has been used for navigation purposes, helping travelers determine which way is south. *http://www.enchantedlearning.com/subjects/astronomy/activities/dots/crux/. 14.01.2011.* The Kappa Crucis Cluster, also known as the Jewel Box, was given its nickname by the English astronomer John Herschel in the 1830s because the striking colour contrasts of its pale blue and orange stars seen through a telescope reminded Herschel of a piece of exotic jewellery. - *http://www.astronomy.com/en/sitecore/content/Home/News-Observing/News/2009/10/Opening%20up%20a%20colorful%20cosmic%20jewel%20box.aspx. 14.01.2011.*
Jewelled Handle - On the north west side of the moon lies an area called *Mare Imbrium* (The Sea of Showers), which contains a mountain range called Jura, and is more or less circular in shape. Its diameter is 800 miles and sweeps round in a semi-circle, and at the bottom of which is the *Sinus Iridium*, (Bay of Rainbows). When the Sun is setting or rising, it catches the mountain tops, leaving the floor in shadow, producing the effect often called the 'Jewelled Handle'. It is said to be a magnificent sight! - edited extract from *The Universe, Patrick Moore*,

"...Jewelled door handle fixed underneath" - This refers to an actual chair that was modified by Salvador Dali. He replaced the chairs leather seat with chocolate, screwed a golden Louis xv door-knob under one leg, and placed another leg in a glass of beer - *Taschen books.1994. ISBN 3-8228-9326-9.*

Ke tha geras - walk away,/buzz off, etc. (18th Century Cornish)
'Meditation Rose', *(Rosa Meditativa) 1958 - a paintng by Salvador Dali.*

Moon gardening - It is believed plants respond to the same gravitational pull of tides that affect the oceans, which alternately stimulates root and leaf growth. Seeds sprout more quickly, plants grow vigorously and at a higher rate, harvests are larger and appear not to go to seed as fast. Moon gardening has been practiced for hundreds of years, and is considered a perfect complement to organic gardening because it is more effective in non-chemically treated soil. 'Just as the moon pulls the tides in the oceans, it also pulls upon the subtle bodies of water, causing moisture to rise in the earth, which encourages growth. The highest amount of moisture is in the soil at this time, and tests have proven that seeds will absorb the most water at the time of the full moon'. - *http://www.gardeningbythemoon.com/- 14.01.2011.*   "The Moon's quarters are referred to as the First, Second, Third and Fourth Quarters, and you will also find them referred to as New Moon, First Quarter, Full Moon and Last Quarter. The planting of seeds in the proper quarter of the moon's life, the pruning of trees, the fertilizing of plants, and the weeding of the garden all according to the influences of the Moon, when observed and practiced correctly, will prove the validity of this gardening method to the gardener year after year, by producing the strongest, most productive vegetables and flowers. *John Harris - http://www.coloradomoongarden.net/Moon_Phases___Planting.html. 17.01.2011.*

Organic production - pesticides are severely restricted, instead a nutrient-rich soil is developed to grow strong healthy crops and encourage wildlife to help control pests and disease. Artificial chemical fertilisers are prohibited, instead organic farmers develop a healthy, fertile soil by growing and rotating a mixture of crops using clover to fix nitrogen from the atmosphere. *http://www. soilassociation.org/Whyorganic/Whatisorganic/tabid/206/Default.aspx. 14.01.2011.*
A healthy soil is the basis for growing healthy plants and healthy food. The soil is full of life – worms, fungi, bacteria and other microscopic creatures – which create its structure and fertility. When looking after your soil organically you will be improving the diversity, and supporting the activity, of these vital creatures. *http://www.gardenorganic.org.uk/pdfs/Organic-Gardening-Guidelines-2010.pdf.14.01.2011.*

Theobroma Cacao - Cocoa
Theobroma Cacao -Luna Rainbowus, Organicus - Moon Rainbow Cocoa, Organic - a ficticious variety named for this story only.

How the story of Sparkle Puss came about:

I have always enjoyed writing about my daily observations especially when travelling. In 2006 I acquired a kitten from a neighbour. I'd always wanted two kittens so that I could call them either Galaxy & Mars or Frankincense & Myrrh. I named the kitten Frankincense and abbreviated it to Insie. She's a striking cat and with her amusing and intelligent nature, she soon started to inspire some writing along with some drawings. I initially started e-mailing one of my sisters, Susie, keeping her updated with 'the Insie antics.' With the drawings developing and the Insie antics growing, it seemed to be a natural progression to put it all into a story. I have a workbench where I make jewellery using glitter and rhinestones. I became aware that Insie started to sparkle with the glitter that she inadvertently picked up in her fur. In 2007 the story of 'Sparkle Puss' began.

Artists Biography:

Looking for new inspiration in 2002, I moved from London to Penzance. After an 18 year career in freelance film & TV animation including for Walt Disney, I returned to study, in Cornwall, which included Horticulture, followed by Complementary Health Therapies. The Horticulture course incorporated my other passions outside of art including; organic production, ethnobotany and rainforests. I had been captivated by cocoa since childhood, the golden pods were of immense fascination having seen them illustrated at school by way of a 2 dimensional pod made of card, that opened out into several layers to reveal its contents. That image registered with me very strongly at 5 yrs old. In the 1980's my awarensess of the environment was growing, and in 1990 I read a book called 'In the Rainforest' by Catherine Caulfield that captured my imagination so vividly I have been compelled to support rainforests ever since. In 1991 I visited a rainforest in Trinidad. Writing my college course assignments revealed even more to me the extraordinary & intriguing biodiversity of the rainforests. I also believe that organic production is the better way to farm.

With my interest in chocolate, over the years, I have gradually been refining my chocolate palette and purchases. It's very important to me to know that the chocolate I'm buying is organic and or fairly traded.

In 2006 I started searching the internet for a small organic cocoa farm to get involved with. In 2007 just by chance I came across a developing organic cocoa project in the Bolivian rainforest. I have been corresponding with them since December 2007 and in 2008 the project manager, Hugo, came to Europe and visited me in Penzance. He was very inspired by Cornwall and we discussed making a chocolate bar to go with 'Sparkle Puss', using his organic criollo cocoa beans. Meanwhile, I am producing organic Sparkle Puss chocolate truffles made with organic cacao from a UK producer.